Venus

by Nancy Loewen

Consultant:
Kenneth F. Kitchell Jr., Ph.D.
Department of Classics
University of Massachusetts, Amherst

RiverFront Books

an imprint of Franklin Watts
A Division of Grolier Publishing
New York   London   Hong Kong   Sydney
Danbury, Connecticut

RiverFront Books
http://publishing.grolier.com

Printed in the United States of America.
Published simultaneously in Canada.

Library of Congress Cataloging-in-Publication Data
Loewen, Nancy, 1964–
Venus/by Nancy Loewen.
p. cm.—(Greek and Roman mythology)
Includes bibliographical references and index.
Summary: Surveys classical mythology, discussing the relationship between Greek and Roman myths, and describes the birth and life of the goddess Venus.
ISBN 0-7368-0050-6
1. Venus (Roman deity)—Juvenile literature. [1. Venus (Roman deity) 2. Mythology, Roman. 3. Mythology, Greek.] I. Title. II. Series.
BL820.V5L64 1999
291.2'114—dc21

98-35113
CIP
AC

Editorial Credits

Christy Steele, editor; Clay Schotzko/Icon Productions, cover designer; Timothy Halldin, illustrator; Sheri Gosewisch, photo researcher

Photo Credits

Archive Photos, 11, 31, 33; Lambert, 38; Pepperfoto, 41
Art Resource, cover; Erich Lessing, 14, 17, 18, 20; Scala, 26-27; The Andy Warhol Foundation for Visual Arts, 28
Corbis-Bettmann, 22
NASA, 34
Unicorn Stock Photos/Marie Mills, 25
Visuals Unlimited/Bruce Berg, 4; Jeff Greenbert, 36; David Sieren, 42
William B. Folsom, 46

Table of Contents

Chapter 1 About Mythology 5

Chapter 2 Young Venus 15

Chapter 3 Loves of Venus 21

Chapter 4 The Goddess of Love 29

Chapter 5 Mythology in the Modern World 35

Words to Know 43

To Learn More 44

Useful Addresses 45

Internet Sites 47

Index 48

This book is illustrated with photographs of statues, paintings, illustrations, and other artwork about mythology by artists from both ancient and modern times.

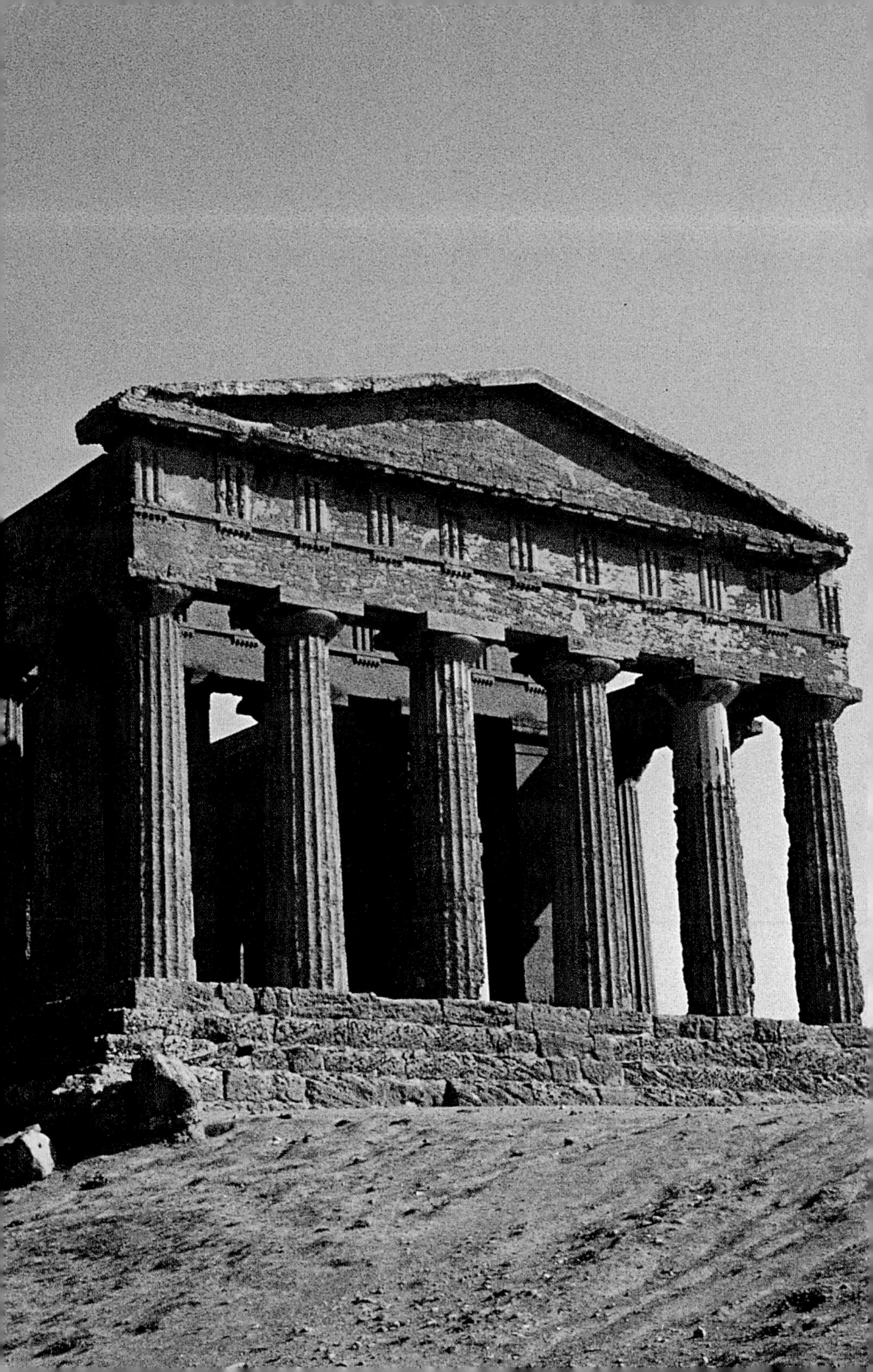

Chapter One

About Mythology

People in Greece and Rome told stories as early as 2000 B.C. These stories served an important purpose in ancient communities. People used the stories to explain human history and the natural world.

Greek and Roman people believed gods, goddesses, heroes, and monsters controlled the world. These powerful beings were the main characters in the stories ancient people told.

The stories created a sense of order and understanding in the lives of ancient Greeks and Romans. Most people did not know much about science. The stories used characters people could understand to make the world seem more familiar and less frightening.

Today, scholars call these stories myths. Myths once served important purposes. But no

Greek and Roman people worshiped the characters from their stories. Remains of some temples they built for the gods and goddesses still stand today.

one believes in myths any longer. Scientists help people explain the natural world. The collection of the hundreds of Greek and Roman myths is called classical mythology.

Quest myths describe a character's search for something. The characters must face danger to complete their quests.

Explanation myths tell how things happen. According to one Greek myth, a huge bull that lived underground caused earthquakes. Other myths explained the groupings of the stars in the sky and the changing of the seasons.

History of Mythology

The myths in classical mythology started in both ancient Greece and Rome. Greece is a country in what is now Europe. The Roman Empire was a group of countries under Roman rule. Rome was the capital city of the Roman Empire. Rome is in what is now Italy.

Greeks were among the first people to tell stories about gods, goddesses, heroes, and monsters. Greeks told their stories to the next generation. In this way, myths were passed on for thousands of years.

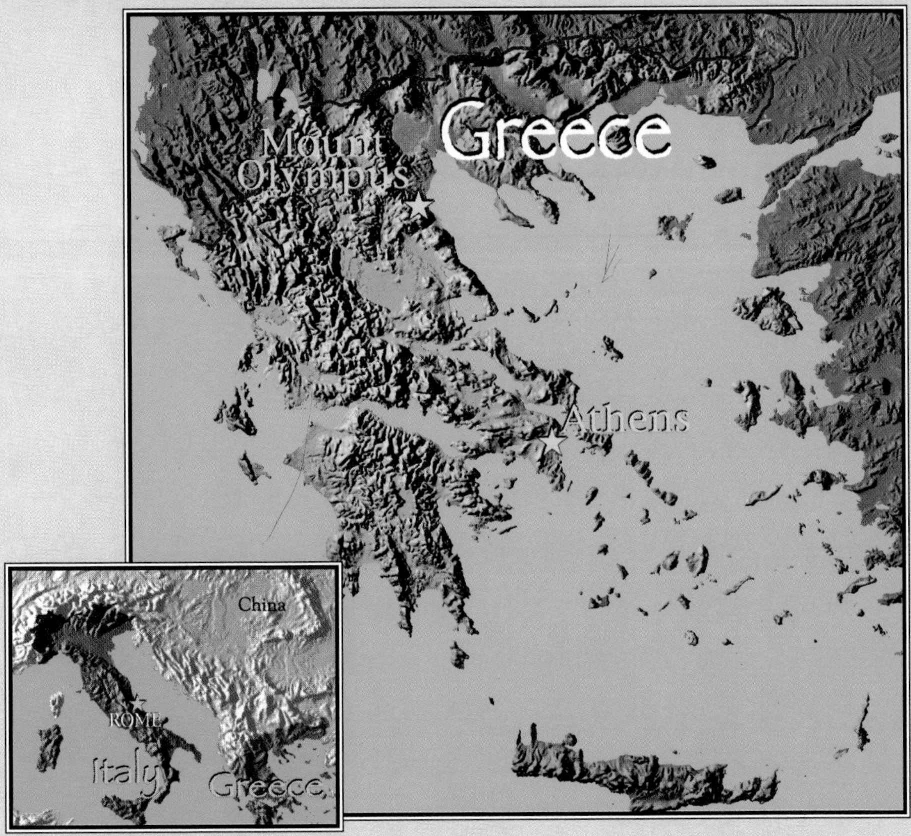
Greece
Mount Olympus
Athens
China
ROME
Italy
Greece

Rome conquered Greece in about 100 B.C. The Romans adopted some Greek beliefs. Greek myths were popular among Romans.

Romans began to tell their own myths. Some of the Roman myths were similar to the Greek myths. Many of the Roman gods and goddesses had the same powers as Greek gods and goddesses. Romans gave their characters different names.

Gods and Goddesses
of Greek and Roman Mythology

Zeus (Greek)   Jupiter (Roman)
King of the gods and goddesses

Hera (Greek)   Juno (Roman)
Queen of the gods and goddesses

Athena (Greek)   Minerva (Roman)
Goddess of wisdom and war

Apollo (Greek)   No Roman Name
God of beauty, the Sun, prophecy, and healing

Artemis (Greek)   Diana (Roman)
Goddess of the moon and the hunt

Hermes (Greek)   Mercury (Roman)
God of business and commerce; messenger to Zeus

Aphrodite (Greek)   Venus (Roman)
Goddess of love, beauty, and fertility

Dionysus (Greek)   Bacchus (Roman)
God of wine, song, and drama

Poseidon (Greek)   Neptune (Roman)
God of the seas

Hades (Greek)   Pluto (Roman)
God of the Underworld

Demeter (Greek)   Ceres (Roman)
Goddess of agriculture

Ares (Greek)   Mars (Roman)
God of war

Hephaestus (Greek)   Vulcan (Roman)
God of fire

Hestia (Greek)   Vesta (Roman)
Goddess of the hearth

For example, the Greek goddess of love, beauty, motherhood, and marriage was Aphrodite. The Roman goddess of love was Venus. Venus and Aphrodite had the same powers and duties. Both Romans and Greeks told similar stories about Venus and Aphrodite. This book uses the Roman names of the mythological characters.

Storytellers memorized myths and told the stories to the people. Most people living in ancient Greece and the Roman Empire did not know how to write and read. They did not write the myths down on paper. Instead, people learned the myths from the storytellers.

Storytellers sometimes added new ideas to make the myths seem more exciting. Some storytellers told the myths incorrectly. Many versions of the myths exist today because storytellers told the myths in different ways.

History of the Gods

Chaos gave birth to the oldest god, Heaven, and the oldest goddess, Earth. Heaven and Earth had many children. Some of their children had 150 hands. Heaven and Earth also had cyclopes.

These giants had only one eye in the middle of their foreheads. Earth also gave birth to several powerful giants called titans.

Heaven was cruel. He did not like his cyclops children. So he locked them underground. Heaven's son Cronus did not like his father. Cronus wanted to rule the world. So Cronus conquered Heaven and became the ruler.

Cronus married the titan Rhea. Rhea gave birth to six children. Cronus did not want his children to conquer him. He ate all of them except Jupiter. Rhea gave Cronus a rock to eat when Jupiter was born. She hid Jupiter from Cronus.

Jupiter grew up. He disguised himself and gave Cronus a special medicine. The medicine freed the other children from Cronus' body. Jupiter conquered Cronus and the other titans with the help of his brothers and sisters. Jupiter set the cyclopes and 150-handed giants free. He locked Cronus and the other titans underground. Jupiter became king of the gods.

Some of Cronus and Rhea's children married each other and had children. Their children were gods and goddesses too.

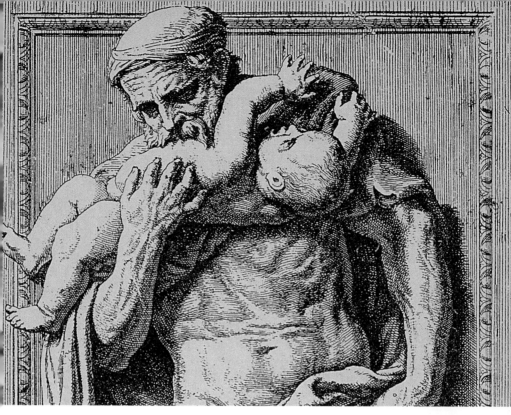

Cronus ate his children so they would not grow up and conquer him.

Gods and Goddesses

Some gods and goddesses were more powerful than others. The gods and goddesses sometimes fought each other to increase their power and rank. Venus was a very powerful goddess.

People believed the powerful gods and goddesses lived on top of Mount Olympus. This mountain is the highest point in Greece. Less important gods and goddesses lived throughout the earth, sky, and sea. Venus lived on Mount Olympus.

The gods and goddesses behaved very much like humans. Venus often became envious of other women's beauty. Venus could also be caring. She often helped unhappy people find love. But unlike humans, Venus had magical powers that were almost unlimited. She was immortal. She would never die.

Religion

Greeks and Romans worshiped the gods and goddesses. Each person worshiped the powerful beings that mattered most to their lives. People who were lonely prayed to Venus for help. They hoped she would help them fall in love with someone.

Greeks and Romans honored the gods and goddesses in many ways. Some built temples to honor their favorite gods or goddesses. People brought offerings of money and food to the temples. Artists painted pictures and made statues of the gods and goddesses for the temples.

Characters in Mythology

Classical mythology contained hundreds of characters. Some characters appeared in many different stories. Other characters were only in a few myths. Most characters belonged to one of the following groups:

Titans: These gods and goddesses were powerful giants. They were the children of Earth and Heaven.

Olympians: These were the main gods in classical mythology. Olympians looked like humans. But they had magic powers. They ruled from the top of Mount Olympus. Jupiter was the head of the Olympians.

Lesser gods: These gods were less powerful than the Olympians. They often were associated with one particular area such as a river or mountain.

Demigods: These were half-god and half-human characters. They had more power than ordinary humans, but were weaker than the gods. Demigods were not immortal.

Monsters: Monsters could be a combination of different animals or of animals and humans. Gods sent monsters to punish people.

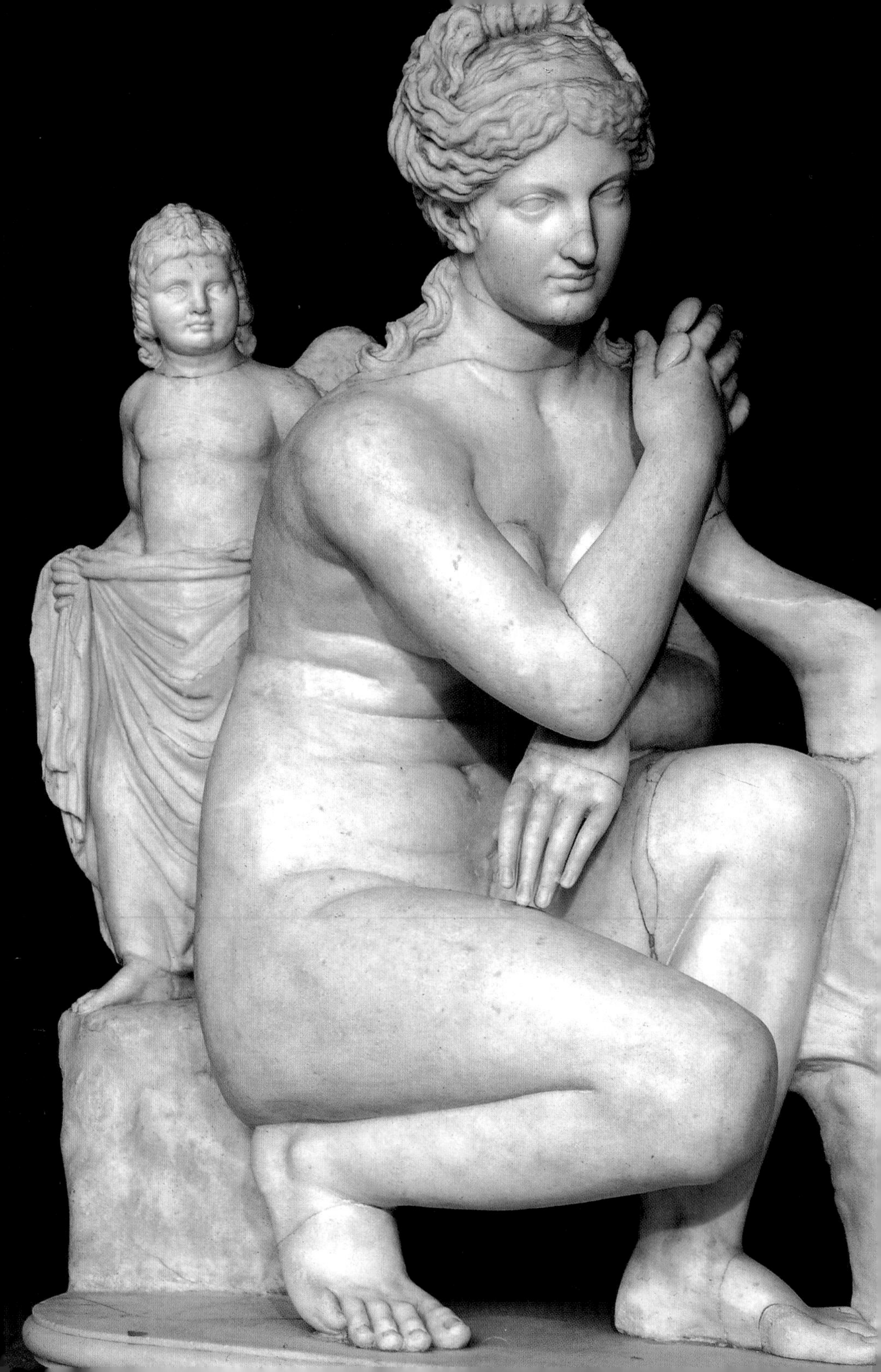

Young Venus

Venus was one of the most popular goddesses in the Roman Empire. People told many stories about her. The stories explained how and why people fall in love.

Ancient Greek and Roman people associated certain objects with Venus. She traveled in a chariot that was pulled by doves. A chariot is a light, two-wheeled cart. She also had a belt called a magic girdle. The girdle made men unable to resist her. But Venus did not need the girdle to make men love her. She was very beautiful. Venus had many children.

Birth of Venus
Venus was born after the battle between Cronus and Heaven. Cronus cut Heaven with a sharp

---

Venus was one of the most popular goddesses in the Roman Empire.

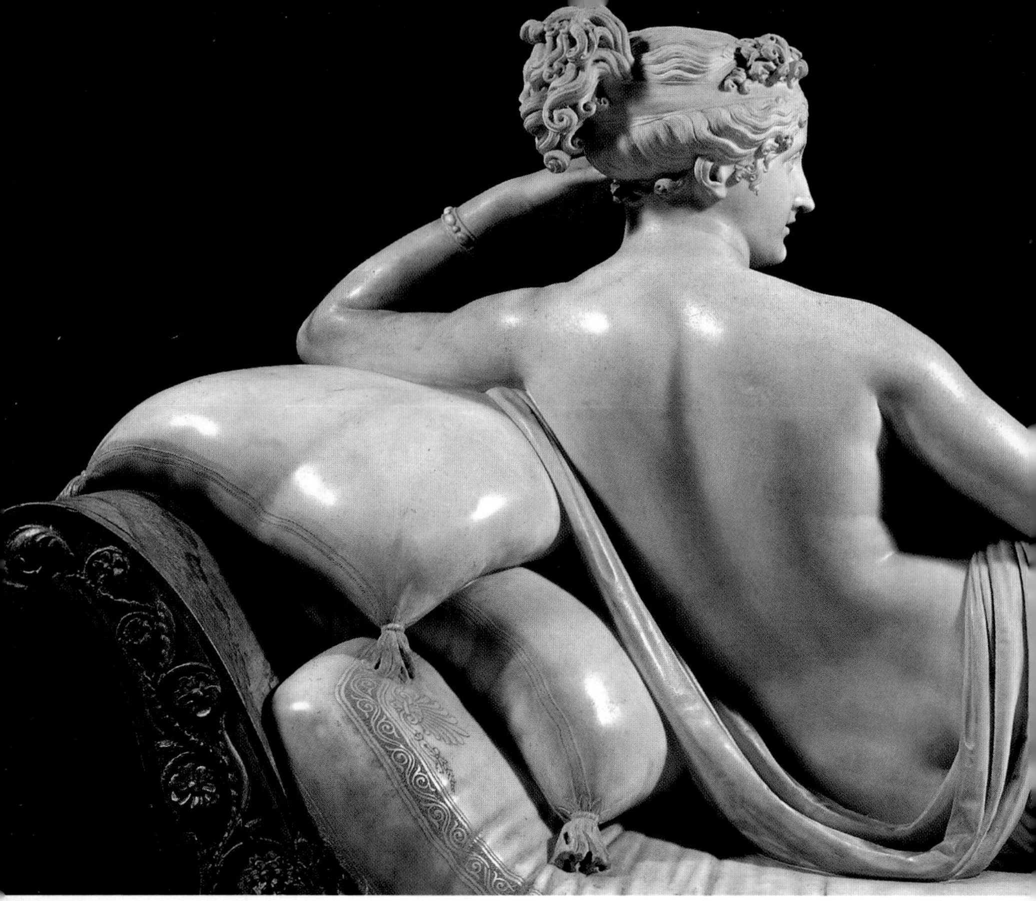

Venus was charming, playful, and beautiful.

sickle. Large drops of Heaven's blood fell into the sea.

The blood turned into white foam that churned in the water. The goddess Venus appeared from the foam. She was fully grown and very beautiful. She washed onto shore in a giant sea shell.

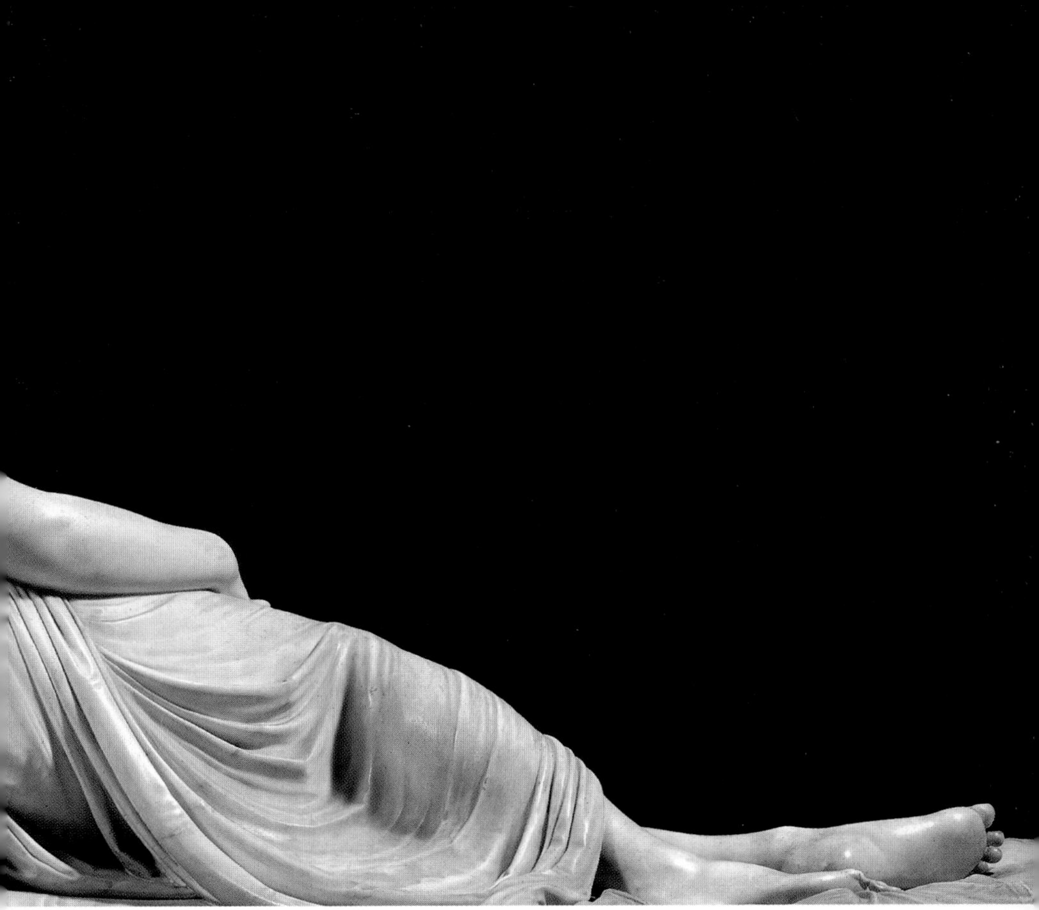

The Seasons greeted Venus at the water's edge. The Seasons were three young goddesses that represented spring, summer, and winter.

The Seasons sensed Venus' power. They knew that she belonged on Mount Olympus. They dressed Venus. They then led her to Mount Olympus.

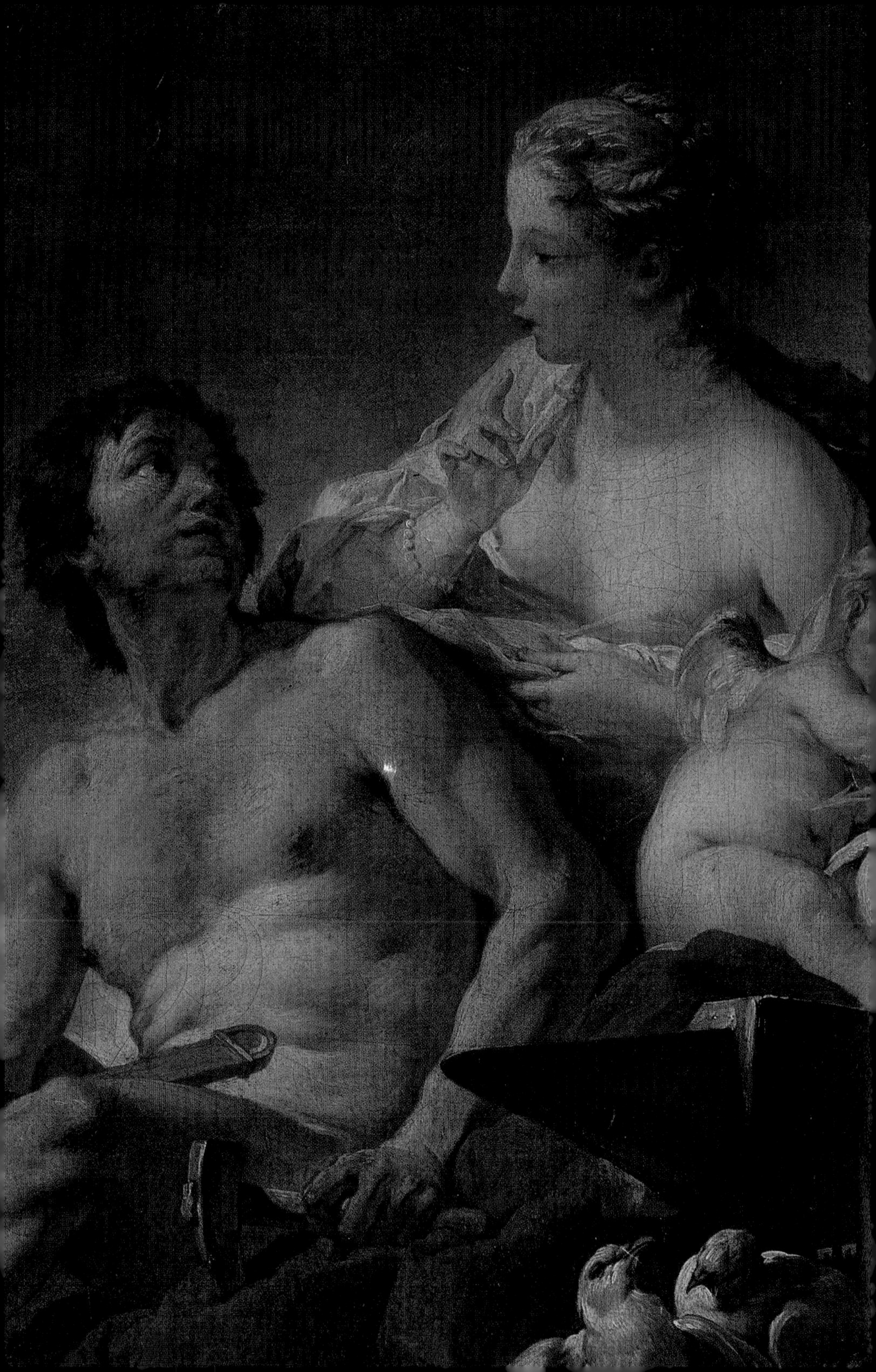

Marriage of Venus

Venus was charming and playful. All the male gods fell in love with her. Jupiter knew that Venus would cause trouble unless she married. The male gods would fight each other to win Venus' favor. Jupiter made Venus marry his son Vulcan. Vulcan was the god of fire and metal.

Vulcan loved Venus. He was faithful, hardworking, and kind. But he also was ugly. Vulcan could not believe that Venus had married him. The other gods could not believe it either.

At first, Venus was unhappy about her arranged marriage. But she soon realized that Vulcan was useful to her. He was a skilled worker who could make metal objects. He made powerful weapons and fancy jewelry for Venus. He even made her magic girdle.

Venus realized that Vulcan was useful to her.

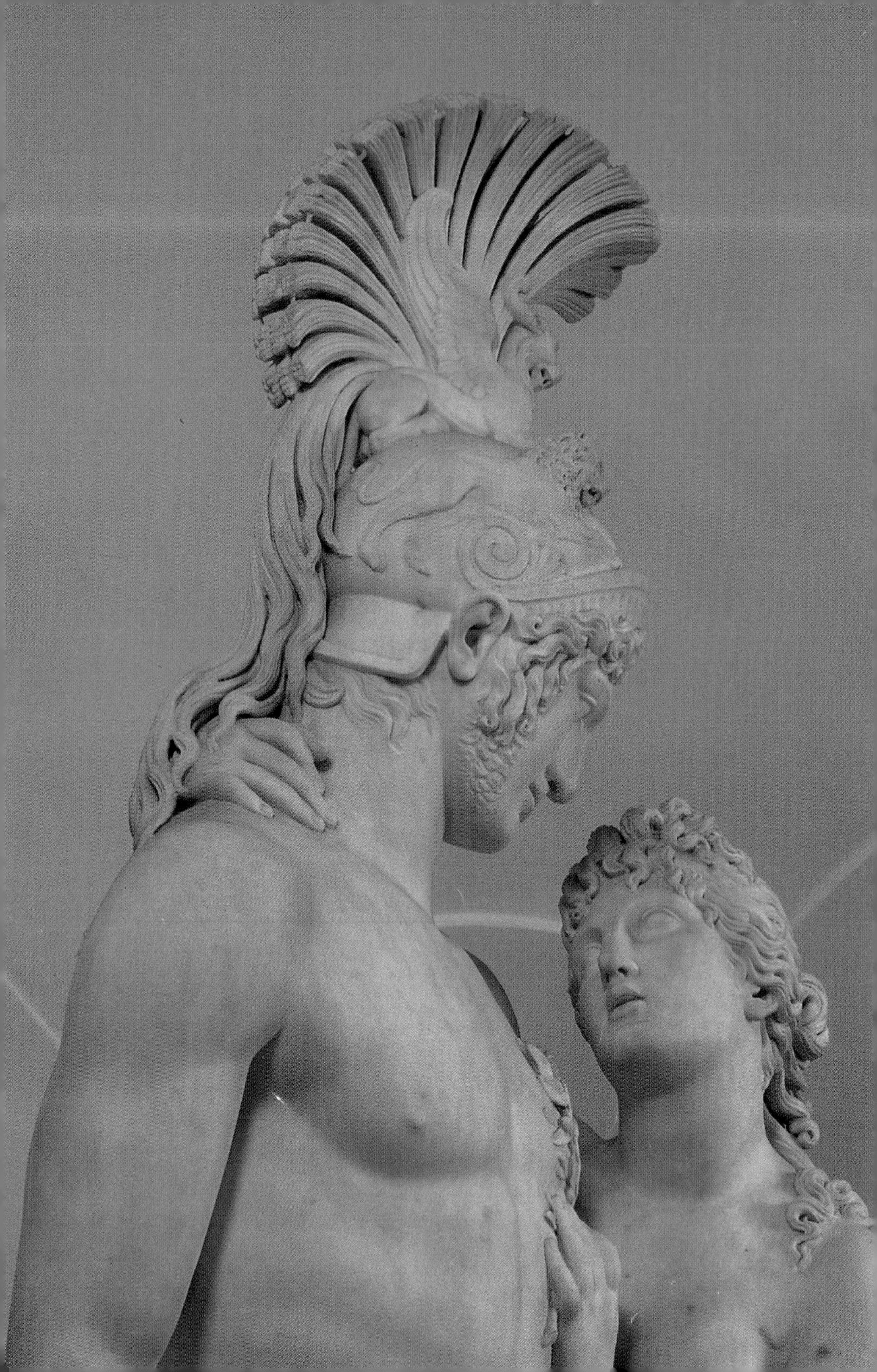

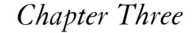

Chapter Three

Loves of Venus

V enus was so beautiful that many men and gods fell in love with her. Even though she was married, Venus sometimes fell in love with them too. Many myths tell about times Venus fell in love.

Vulcan sometimes became angry with Venus. But Venus knew she could do as she pleased. Vulcan loved Venus so much that he always forgave her.

Venus and Mars

Venus fell in love with Mars, the god of war. Venus loved Mars because he was handsome and bold. He enjoyed fighting. Mars and Venus stayed in love for a long time.

Venus loved Mars because he was handsome and bold.

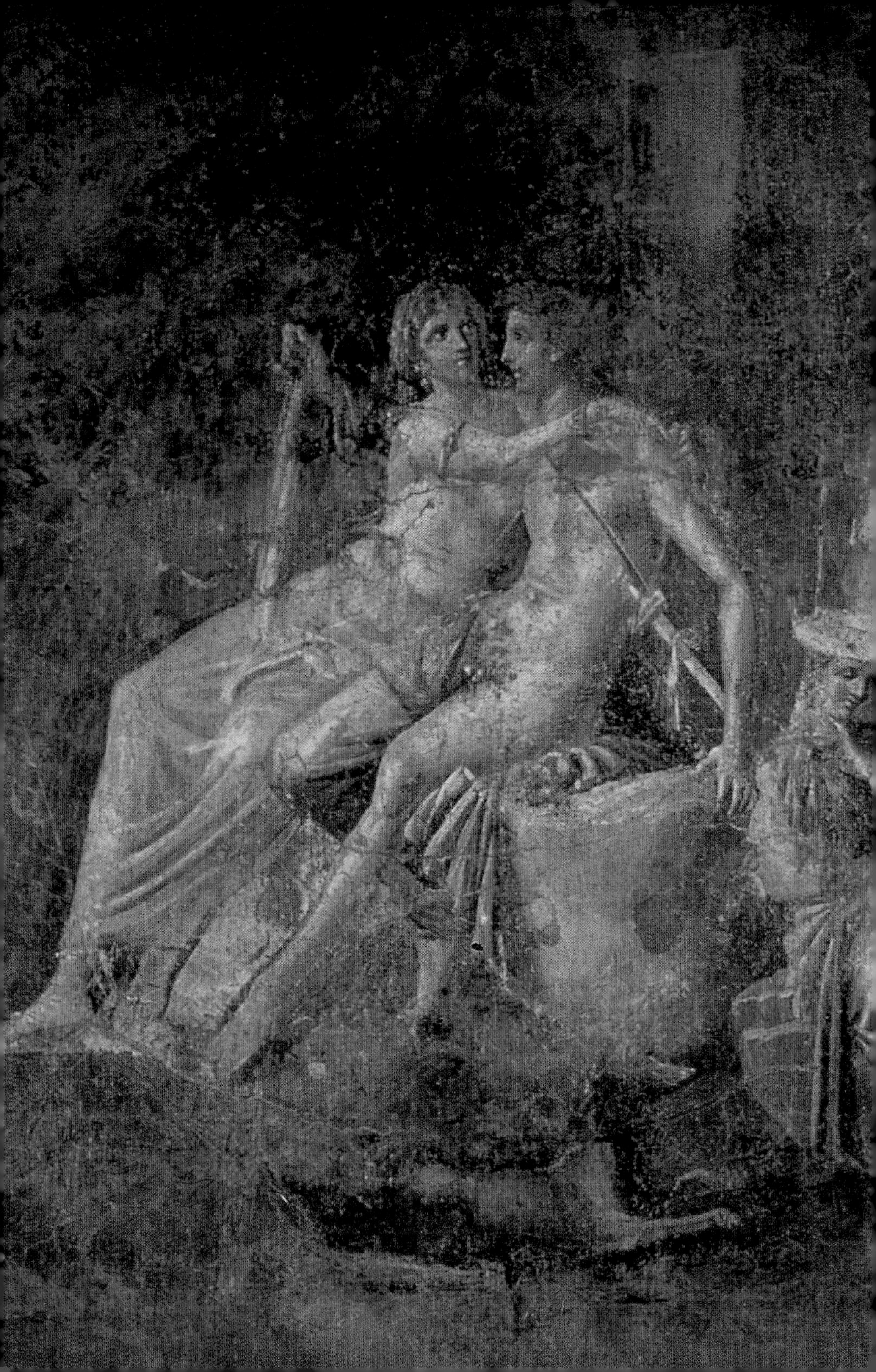

One day, Sol saw Mars and Venus together. Sol was the Sun god. Sol told Vulcan.

Vulcan became angry. He wanted to teach Venus and Mars a lesson. Vulcan wove a magic net made of fine bronze wire. He wanted the net to be strong enough to hold Venus and Mars. The net was hard to see. Vulcan put the net above Venus' bed. He then told Venus that he was going away for a few days.

Mars came over when he thought Vulcan had left. But Vulcan had not really left. He was hiding. He waited for a short time and then pulled a secret cord that dropped the net onto Venus and Mars.

Vulcan called the other Olympian gods. Everyone laughed at Venus and Mars.

Venus and Mars were so embarrassed that they went to separate islands. They stayed away from each other for a long time.

One day, Sol saw Mars and Venus together.

Adonis

Venus fell in love with a mortal man named Adonis. Adonis was so handsome that his appearance amazed both people and gods.

Mars was angry and envious of Venus' love for Adonis. So Mars turned himself into a wild boar and gored Adonis to death with his tusks. A tusk is a long, curved tooth.

Venus wept over Adonis' body. Her tears fell to the earth and became roses. Beautiful flowers called anemones grew from Adonis' blood on the ground.

Adonis went to the Underworld. The Underworld was the home of the dead. Pluto was the god of the Underworld. His wife Proserpina fell in love with Adonis.

Venus traveled to the Underworld. She wanted Adonis to leave with her. Proserpina did not want to let Adonis leave. Venus and Proserpina fought over Adonis.

Venus and Proserpina finally went to Jupiter. They asked Jupiter to decide who would get to

Venus' tears fell on the ground and turned into roses.

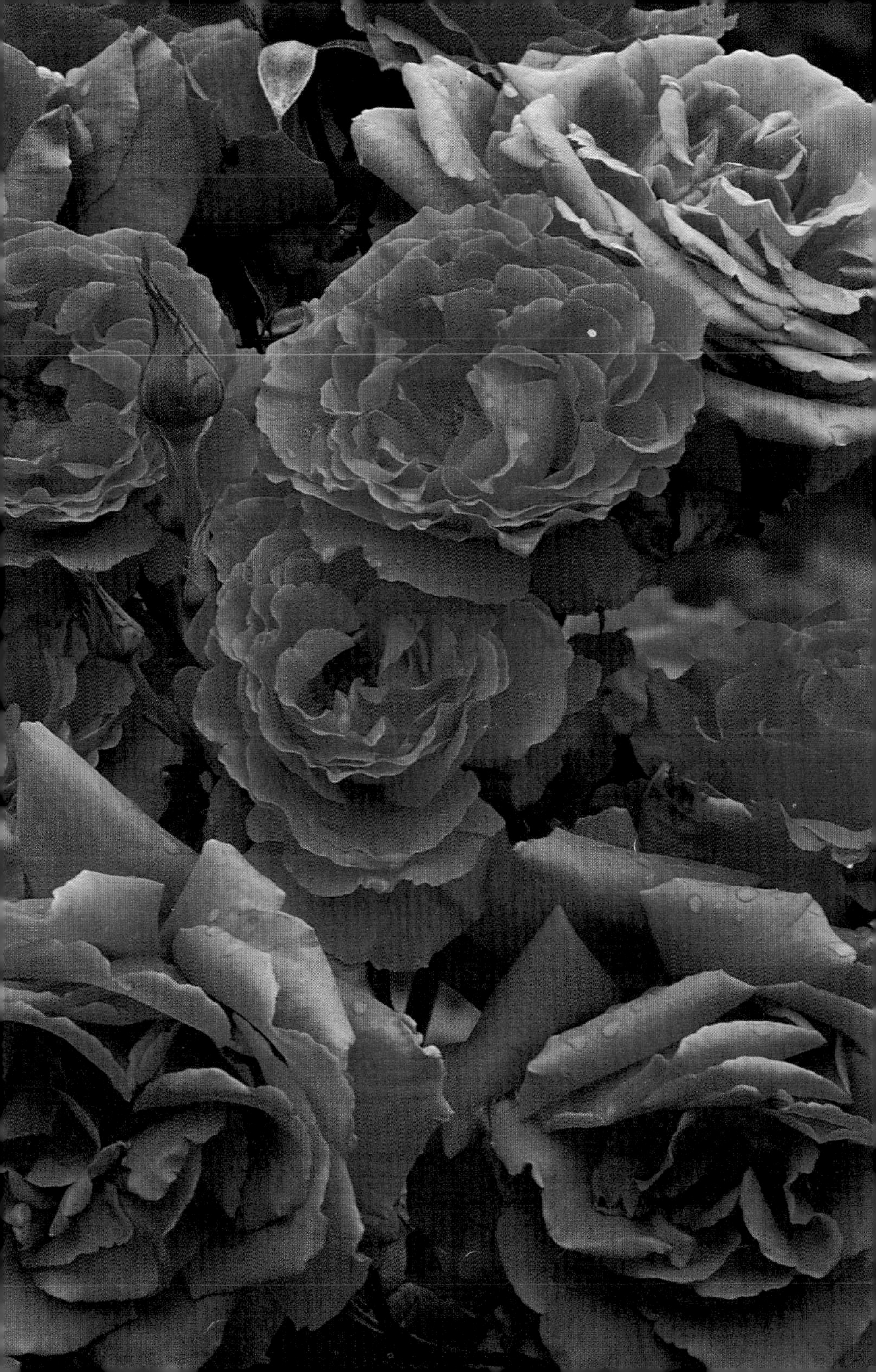

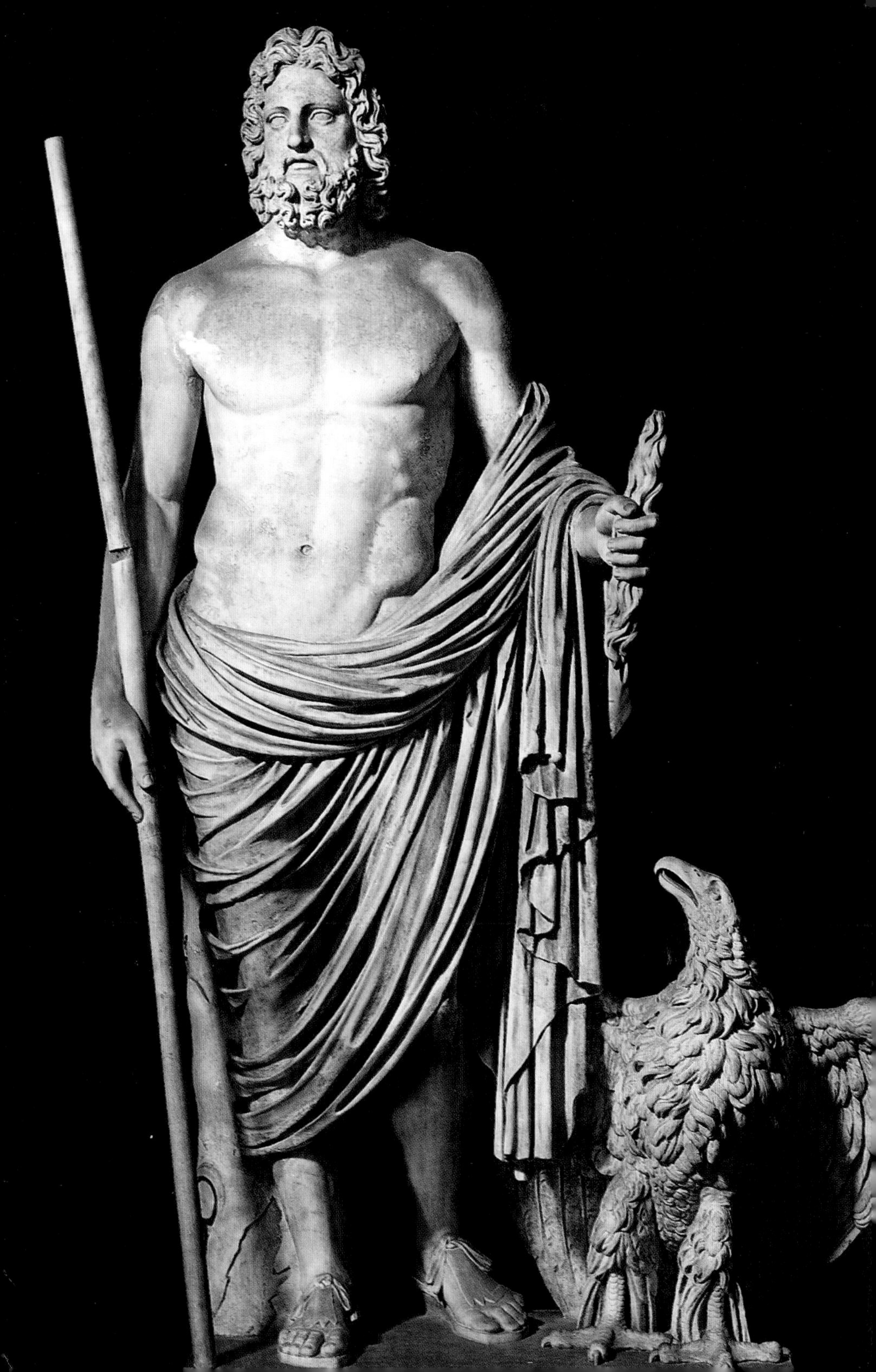

live with Adonis. Venus begged Jupiter to let Adonis return to the earth with her. Meanwhile, Proserpina begged Jupiter to let her keep him in the Underworld.

Jupiter decided to have Adonis split his time between Proserpina and Venus. Adonis would stay with Proserpina for one-third of the year. He would stay with Venus for another one-third of the year. Adonis could stay with whomever he chose for the remaining one-third of the year.

Adonis chose to stay with Venus and not Proserpina. The two goddesses obeyed Jupiter's decision. But they remained enemies.

Jupiter decided to have Adonis split his time between Proserpina and Venus.

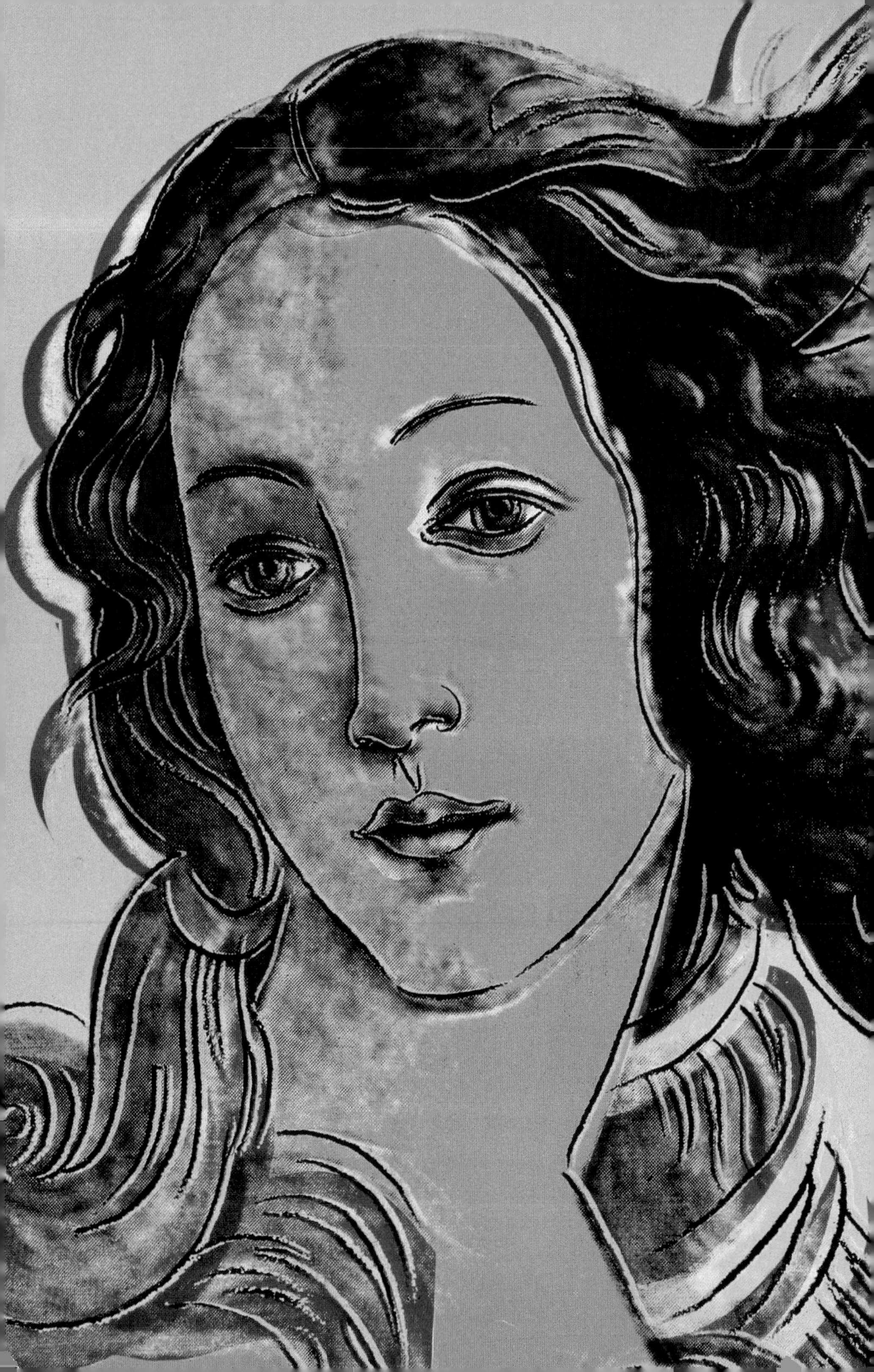

Chapter Four

The Goddess of Love

Venus' job as goddess of love was to help people who were unlucky with love. People would pray to Venus for help. Sometimes Venus answered people's prayers. Many myths tell how Venus helped people.

Pygmalion's Wish

Pygmalion was a king. He created sculptures in his spare time. One day, Pygmalion began shaping a piece of ivory into a statue of a woman. The statue was beautiful. Every detail was perfect. Pygmalion fell in love with the statue. He wanted the statue to be a real woman.

Soon it was time for a yearly festival to honor Venus. Pygmalion went to the festival. He prayed that Venus would send him a woman just like his statue.

Venus helped people who were unlucky with love.

That night, Pygmalion went home and touched the statue's cheek. The cheek felt warm. Venus had granted Pygmalion's wish. The statue came to life.

Pygmalion married the woman he had helped to create. The couple was very happy together.

Hippomenes and Atalanta

Hippomenes was a mortal man in love with a princess named Atalanta. Many other men also wanted to marry Atalanta. But she did not return any man's love. She wanted to spend time alone hunting in the woods.

Atalanta's father wanted her to marry. She promised to marry the first man who could beat her in a race. Atalanta could run so fast that she almost seemed to fly.

Atalanta made one rule for the race. Her father would order soldiers to kill any man who raced against her and lost. Many men raced Atalanta in spite of the rule. All of these men lost the races and their lives.

Venus made Pygmalion's statue come alive.

Hippomenes knew he could not win the race without help. He prayed to Venus. Venus agreed to help him. She gave him three gold apples. She then told him how to use the apples.

Hippomenes challenged Atalanta to a race. Atalanta quickly took the lead once they began racing. Hippomenes threw one of the golden apples on the ground in front of her. Atalanta stopped running and picked up the apple.

Hippomenes took the lead in the race. But Atalanta soon caught up with him. He threw another apple. Atalanta stopped again. Hippomenes threw the last apple as the race was about to end.

Atalanta realized what Hippomenes was doing. But she decided that she loved Hippomenes. She slowed down enough to let him win the race.

Hippomenes and Atalanta married and were very happy together. But they forgot to thank Venus for her help. Venus became angry because the couple was not grateful. She turned them into lions.

Venus became angry because the couple was not grateful.

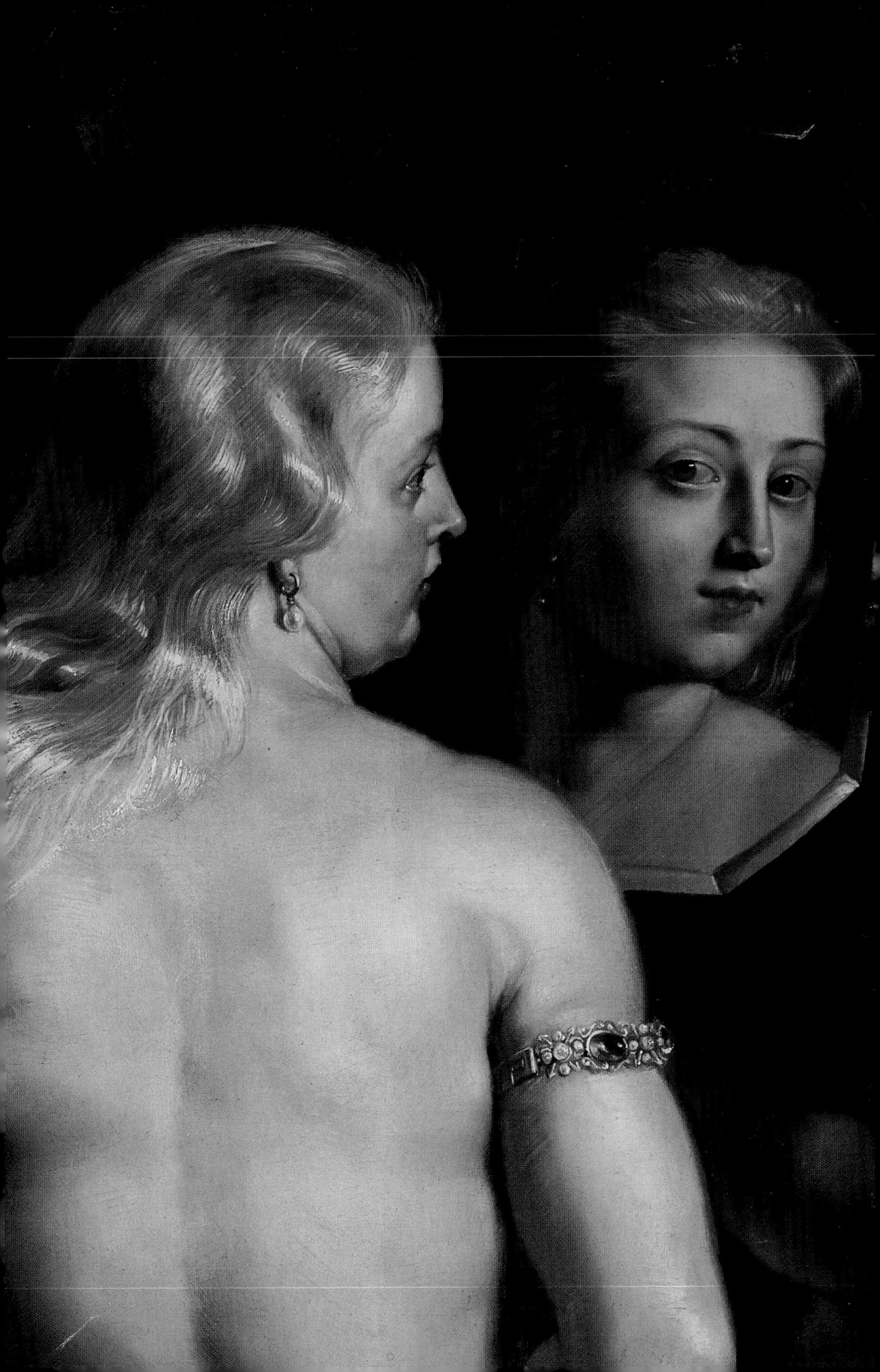

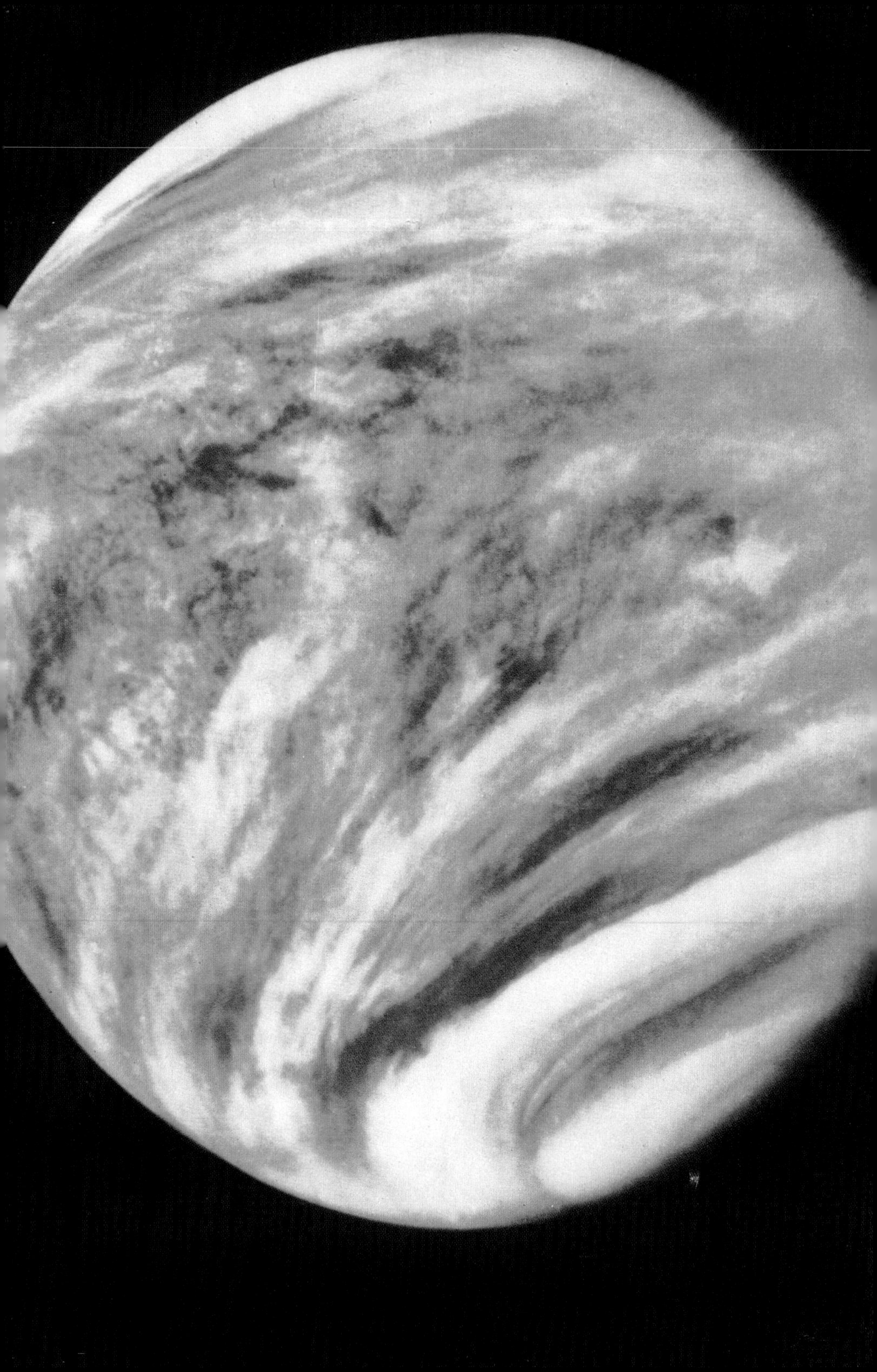

Chapter Five

Mythology in the Modern World

Myths are thousands of years old. But the characters and stories from myths still affect people today. For example, Roman people named planets in our solar system after gods and goddesses from their stories.

The second planet from the sun is named Venus. Early astronomers could see the planet through their telescopes. The astronomers thought the planet was beautiful and named it Venus for the beautiful goddess of love.

Architecture, Books, and Movies

Myths have influenced architecture. Architecture is the planning of buildings. People often create buildings that look like ancient

Early astronomers named the second planet from the Sun Venus for the beautiful goddess of love.

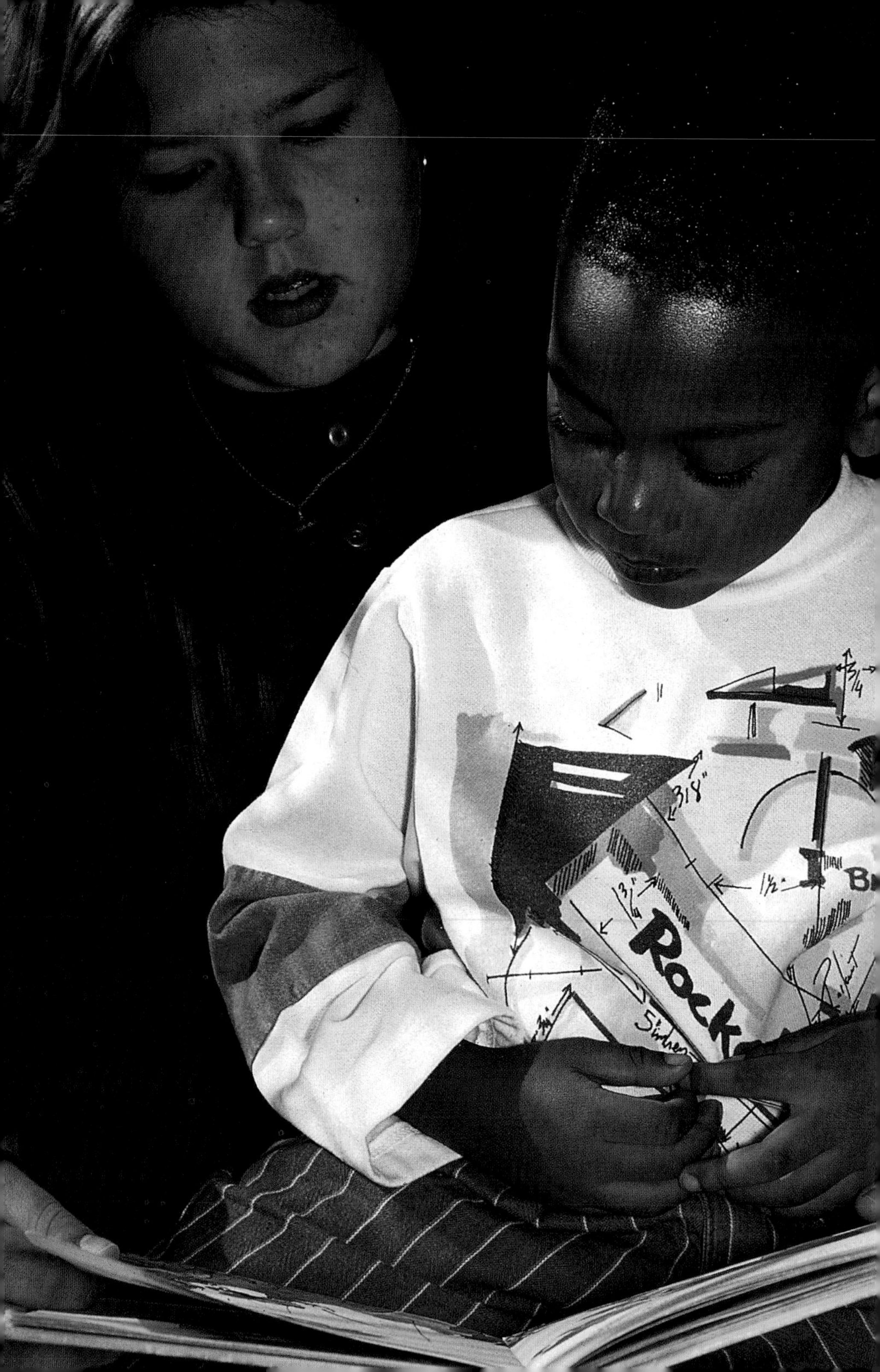
Rock

Greek or Roman temples. These modern buildings have many columns like the temples once had.

Famous books and stories often refer to characters or action from myths. Authors often compare beautiful women in stories with the goddess Venus. People today still enjoy reading myths about Venus. Students often study myths in school.

People sometimes make movies based on myths. *My Fair Lady* is a movie based on the Pygmalion myth. The movie is a story about a professor who teaches a poor young woman to behave like a queen. The professor then falls in love with the woman. The story is similar to Pygmalion's story. Both stories are about people who fall in love with people they helped to create.

Wedding Customs

Many modern wedding customs come from Venus myths. A custom is a special way of doing something.

People today still enjoy reading myths about Venus

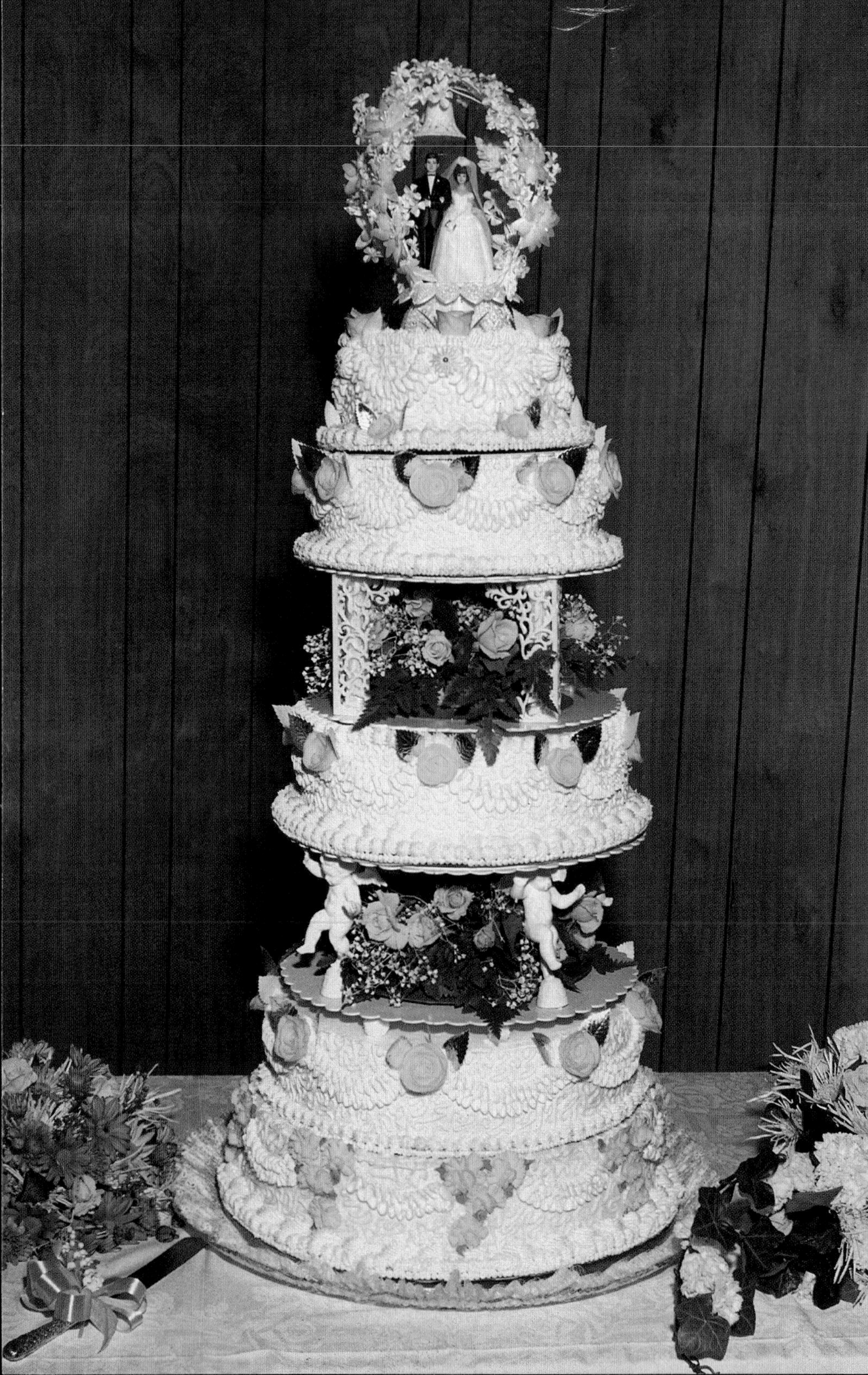

Venus liked the myrtle tree because it reminded her of Adonis. Myrtle flowers are used in wedding bouquets in many different areas of the world.

Roses often are part of wedding flowers or decorations. The first roses grew from the tears Venus shed over Adonis. Red roses now remind people of love and romance.

The dove was Venus' favorite bird. Pictures of doves often are part of wedding decorations.

Cupid

One of Venus' children is well known today. Venus and Mars had a son named Cupid. Cupid was the god of love. He had magical arrows that he shot at people. People fell in love when the arrows hit them. People sometimes say couples have been struck by Cupid's arrows.

Many Valentine's Day decorations have pictures of Cupid on them. Painters often draw Cupid as a chubby little boy with wings. Cards and candy boxes also have images of Cupid on them.

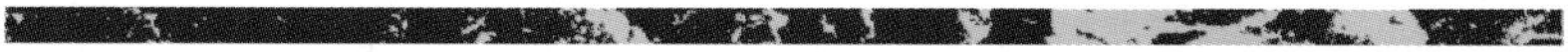

Roses often are a part of wedding flowers or decorations.

The Test of Time

Romance and magic fill the myths about Venus. But the myths were more than good stories. Myths made Greek and Roman people feel connected to each other and to their past. Venus myths show what ancient people believed about love.

The world has changed since the days myths were created in ancient Greece and Rome. Few people worship the gods and goddesses in mythology.

People continue to read classical mythology. Adventure, love, magic, and surprise fill the pages of myths. The myths help readers understand the feelings of people who lived thousands of years ago.

Valentine's Day decorations often have images of Cupid and roses on them.

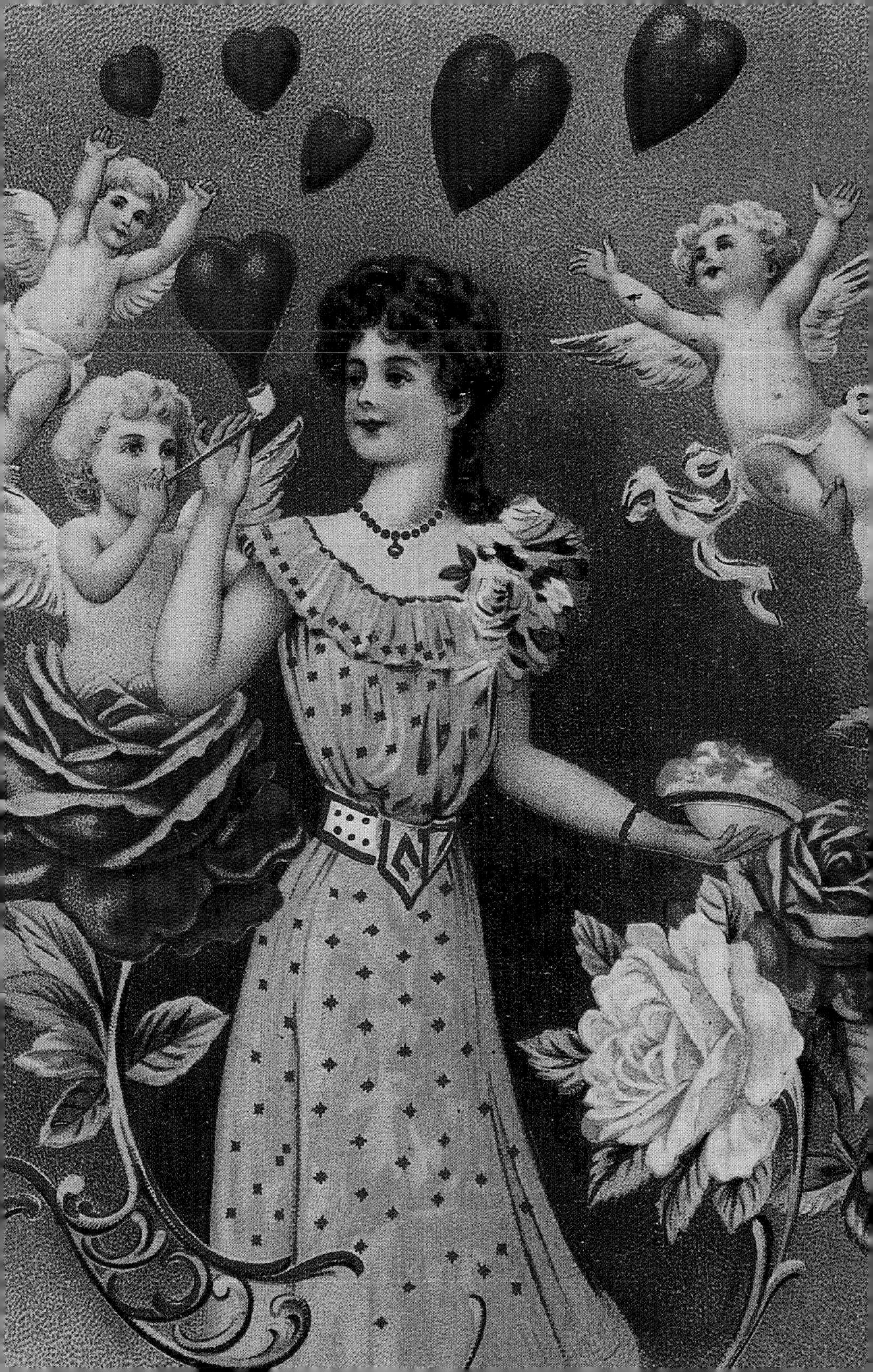

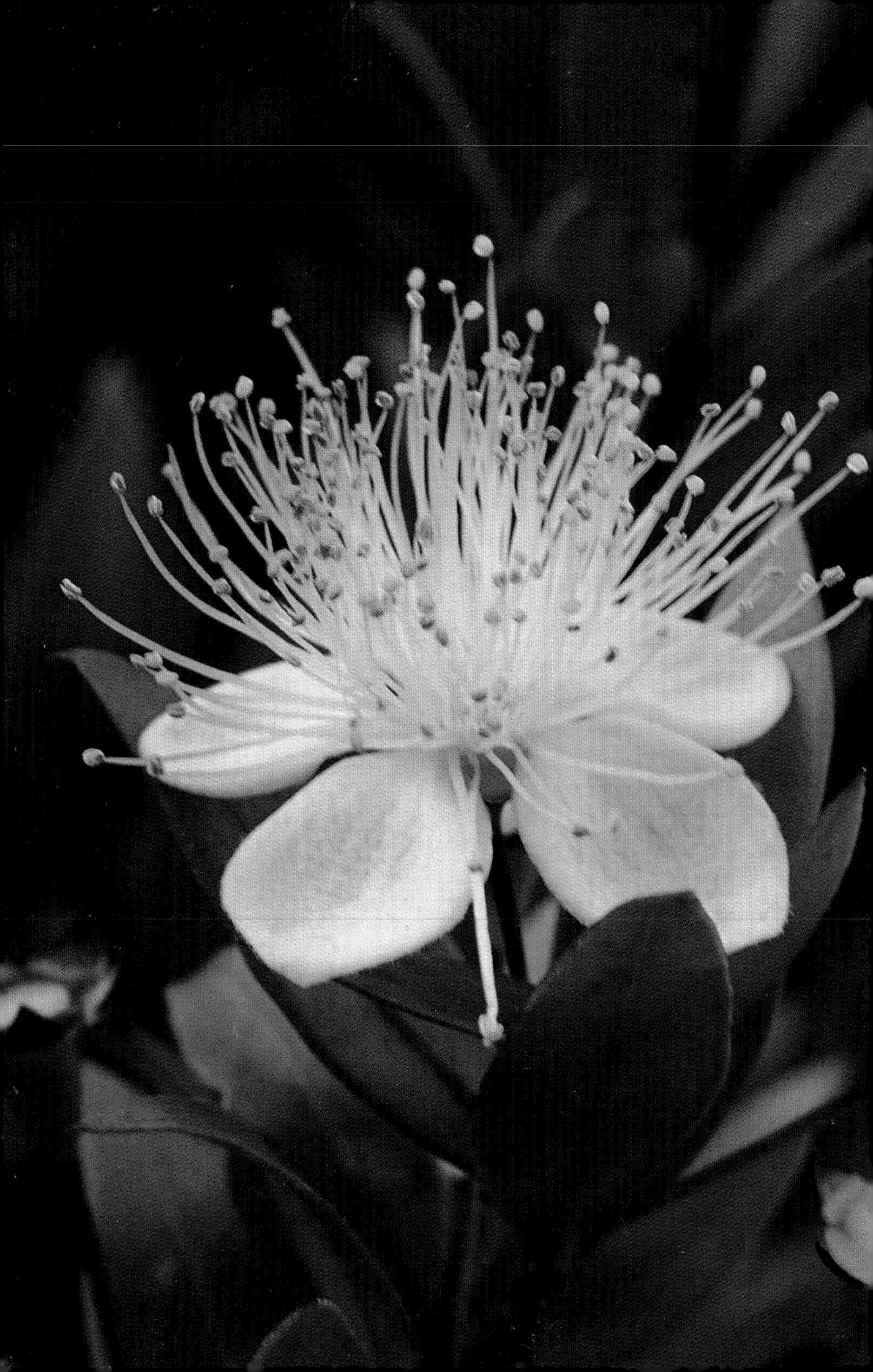

Words to Know

bouquet (boh-KAY)—an arrangement of flowers

chariot (CHA-ree-uht)—a light, two-wheeled cart pulled by horses

custom (KUHSS-tuhm)—a special way of doing something

cyclops (SYE-clahpss)—a giant with one eye in the middle of its forehead

girdle (GUR-duhl)—a belt

immortal (i-MOR-tuhl)—having the ability to live forever

myth (MITH)—a story with a purpose; myths often describe quests or explain natural events.

sickle (SIK-uhl)—a long, curved blade attached to a short handle

Myrtle flowers are used in wedding bouquets in many different countries.

To Learn More

Geringer, Laura. *Atalanta: The Wild Girl.* New York: Scholastic, 1997.

Hull, Robert. *Roman Stories.* New York: Thomson Learning, 1994.

McCaughrean, Geraldine. *Greek Myths.* New York: Margaret McElderry Books, 1993.

Nardo, Don. *Greek and Roman Mythology.* San Diego, Calif.: Lucent Books, 1998.

Williams, Marcia. *Greek Myths for Young Children.* Cambridge, Mass.: Candlewick Press, 1992.

Useful Addresses

American Classical League
Miami University
Oxford, OH 45056-1694

American Philological Association
John Marincola, Secretary/Treasurer
19 University Place, Room 328
New York, NY 10003-4556

Classical Association of the Middle West and South
Gregory Daugherty, Secretary/Treasurer
Department of Classics
Randolph-Macon College
Ashland, VA 23005

Ontario Classical Association
2072 Madden Boulevard
Oakville, ON L6H 3L6
Canada

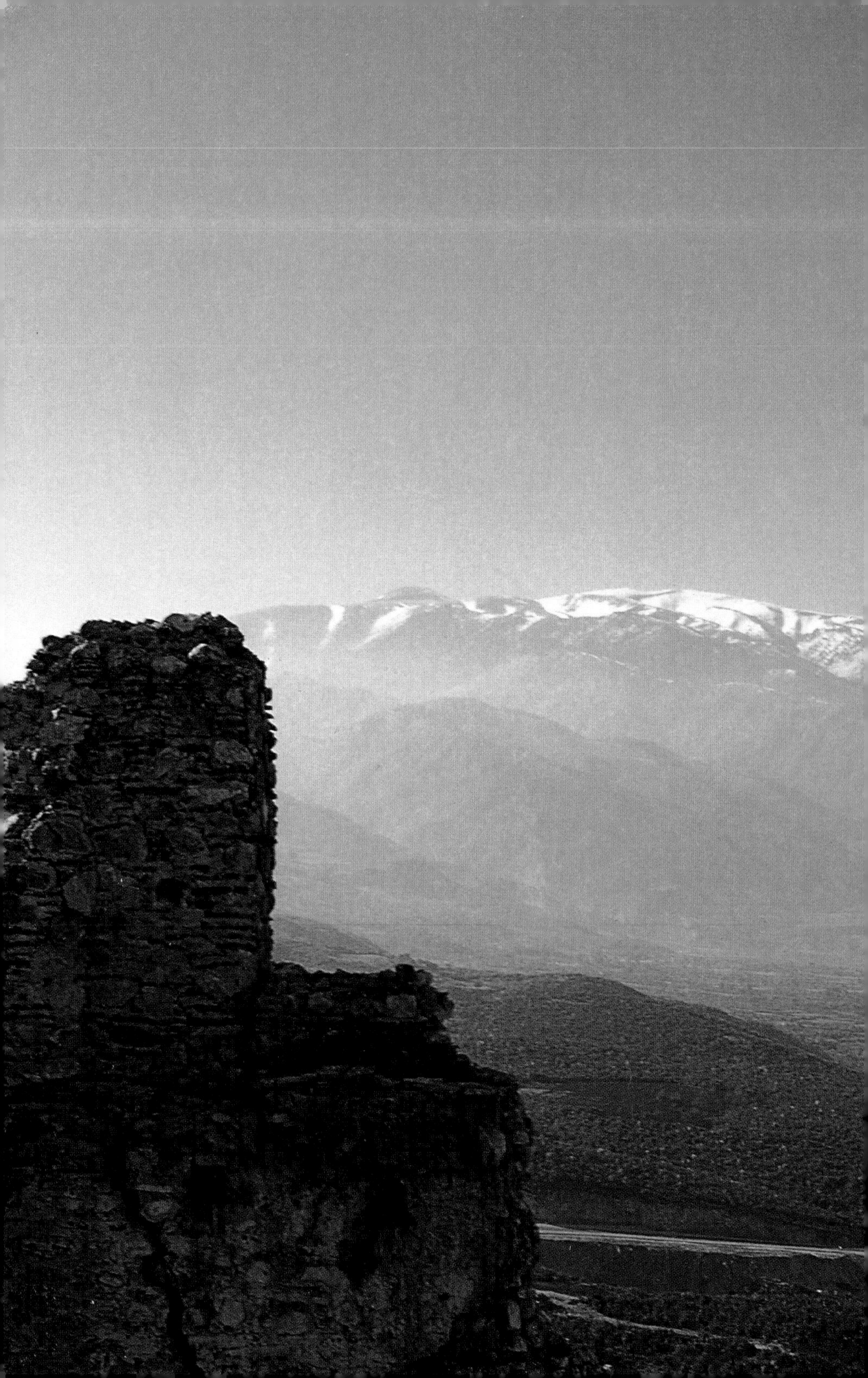

Internet Sites

The Book of Gods, Goddesses, Heroes, and Other Characters of Mythology
http://www.cybercomm.net/~grandpa/gdsindex.html

Encyclopedia Mythica
http://www.pantheon.org/mythica/areas

Mythology
http://www.windows.umich.edu/mythology/mythology.html

Myths and Legends
http://pubpages.unh.edu/~cbsiren/myth.html

The Perseus Project
http://www.perseus.tufts.edu/

World Mythology: Ancient Greek and Roman
http://www.artsMIA.org/mythology/ancientgreekandroman.html

People believed the powerful gods and goddesses lived on top of Mount Olympus.

Index

Adonis, 24, 27, 39
Aphrodite, 9
Atalanta, 30, 32

Cronus, 10
Cupid, 39
cyclops, 9, 10

dove, 15, 39

explanation myths, 6

golden apples, 32

Heaven, 9
Hippomenes, 30, 32

magic girdle, 15, 19
Mount Olympus, 11, 12, 16

My Fair Lady, 37

Proserpina, 24, 27
Pygmalion, 29-30, 37

Rhea, 10
Roman Empire, 6, 7, 9, 15
roses, 24, 39

Seasons, 16
Sol, 23

titans, 10

Valentine's Day, 39
Vulcan, 16, 19, 21, 23

wedding, 37, 39